HARD ASSET

A CLUB ALTURA SHORT STORY

Kym Grosso

MT Carvin Publishing
West Chester, Pennsylvania

Editor: Julie Roberts
Cover Design: Cover Me Darling
Photographer: Wooden Gate Productions
Cover Model: Jase Dean
Formatting: Jason Anderson, Polgarus Studio

DISCLAIMER
This book is a work of fiction. The names, characters, locations and events portrayed in this book are a work of fiction or are used fictitiously. Any similarity to actual events, locales, or real persons, living or dead, is coincidental and not intended by the author.

NOTICE
This is an adult erotic romance book with love scenes and mature situations. It is only intended for adult readers over the age of 18.

❧ *Chapter One* ❧

The pounding beat of the music filtered into the street as Evan stepped out of his black Maserati. He brushed past the line of partygoers, flashing the highly coveted silver feather that had been given to VIP guests. Evan Tredioux had secured an invitation to the elite gala through a military buddy who'd recently become a senator. A casual mention of the party over cocktails at a five-thousand-a-head fundraiser had opened possibilities. A few texts later, and he'd been assured an invite.

Dom Marretta, CEO of Tri-Trylle, hosted the lavish, once-a-year event that served to bring together the country's top influencers. From LA to New York, nearly a hundred of the most relevant men and women gathered to celebrate, to see and be seen. Film stars, beacons of industry, scientists, athletes, musicians, and the ultra-interesting all indulged in champagne and top culinary delights.

For weeks, Evan had suspected sensitive data had been systematically stolen from Emerson Industries, where they'd engaged government contracts, developing top-secret state-of-the-art technologies. Discrepancies in dates assigned to the files had raised red flags but he had no proof. Without concrete evidence, he'd been reluctant to alarm his friend and boss, Garrett Emerson, but had made up his mind to go to him tomorrow and tell him everything. Suspecting he'd been followed for the past few days, Evan had planted a thumb drive of sensitive data with a known white hat hacker, Selby Reynolds, who worked for his friend Lars Elliott. Both individuals were highly competent hackers, and most importantly, they could be trusted should he go missing.

It was well known that Dom Marretta had his hands into selling secrets. From gossip to the latest software developments, he stole, traded, and lied, and covered it all up like a pro. Three years ago, Marretta had been implicated in an attempt to steal data from Emerson Industries, but the key witness went missing as did several pieces of evidence, so it never even made it to trial. Evan suspected if he did a little snooping around Dom's personal office in his home, he'd find at least a clue as to who was messing around in their data.

Adding fuel to the fire, Evan had been tipped off by a friend in the government that an asset would be in attendance tonight, but he couldn't say who. It was suspected foreign nationals were planning a meeting and Marretta had his sticky fingers in the pot. Evan didn't know if the suspected targets were in attendance or guilty of planning any crimes against the state. They could have been planning to trade cookie recipes for all he knew, but he suspected they were sharing information regarding stolen data and technologies. If his suspicion was correct, Emerson Industries' own prototypes could be utilized against allied armed forces. Much of their data still reflected theories but it was light years ahead of their adversaries. Given the volatile state of affairs, leaked secrets, even small ones, could aid terrorist attacks.

Arriving fashionably late ensured Evan that the intoxicated host and the partygoers were relaxed into the night, less likely to notice his activities. Successfully passing through the security check, he strolled into the foyer and brushed past a group of men who were speaking in French, discussing their most recent visit to LA. As he stepped into an enormous living room, a dark and sensual mood filtered throughout; muted conversations had been swallowed into the driving bass that reverberated throughout the contemporary space. Dimly lit bubbled glass light fixtures dangled from the ceiling, illuminating a sea of undulating bodies moving to the music.

Evan gave a cool smile, making his way through the crowd. He spotted a perky blonde at the bar, and her presence set off a cautionary alarm. Although he recalled that she'd occasionally skydived with their group, there was nothing particularly remarkable about her that would garner an invitation and he suspected she had ties to Marretta.

As he stepped outside onto the back porch, he scanned the secluded property. Lanterns of various sizes lit up the perfectly manicured lawn. He glanced to a half dozen topless women who floated in the pool upon glittering golden blow-up swans, their incessant laughter echoing into the night.

Evan accepted a glass of champagne offered by a waiter and kept moving, carefully negotiating the room like a shark seeking its prey. More of a whiskey-straight-up sort, he wasn't much for the bubbly, but for tonight, he'd blend. While pretending to watch the seductive mermaids, out of his peripheral vision he caught sight of a third-story window. Shadows danced in the light behind a curtain, alerting him that the party wasn't limited to the first floor. *Interesting.*

As he made his way back toward the living room, he caught sight of the domineering billionaire. At six foot two inches, Dom Marretta was slightly shorter than Evan. Wearing a fitted royal-blue suit, the ruthless host appeared like the dictator he was. But Evan knew otherwise. Although Marretta had never spent a day in jail, he'd been a suspect in thirteen deaths, not to mention the countless missing persons once in his employ. Anyone stupid enough to sue him found their lawsuit quickly dismissed, courtesy of his legal eagles and bought judges.

"Evan." Marretta gave a boisterous wave.

"Dom Marretta. Finally we meet. Thanks so much for the invite, buddy." Evan's lips curled as he approached. Long ago he'd learned to control his emotions. The surge of anger that pulsed through his veins was tempered by the deliberate decision to remain calm. As he extended his hand, Evan's eyes locked on Marretta's, and he forced an easy laugh, appealing to his host's misogynistic tendencies. "Nice work on the pool scene. Those are some sweet birds ya got going on."

"Nothing but breasts. Haha, I knew you'd be a ladies' man."

"That I am. Excellent party."

"It appears we have mutual friends," Dom mentioned casually, ignoring the compliment.

"You know how it is. Leaving the force never breaks bonds. Our brothers are everywhere."

"So I hear. So I hear. Well, whichever friends you have must have the utmost respect for you for mine to trust them. You are aware of the rules?"

"Absolutely." Evan had been briefed. No gifts. No weapons. No smoking. No guests of guests. No fucking the help. And no matter what you see, illegal or not, you look away and keep your fucking mouth shut. Talk about what happened at the party or who you saw, there was a good chance you'd end up missing. Evan nodded and smiled. "No worries. Just here to enjoy the swans."

"Those are some fucking hot swans, yeah? Who's a pretty bird?" He laughed. His attention drifted to a set of redheaded triplets congregating in the foyer. "If you'll excuse me, some fresh ones just flew in and I think they'll be looking to join my flock. Cardinals. Three is my lucky number tonight."

"Enjoy." Evan's smile faded as Dom turned his back to him. Women were a known weakness to the billionaire, his indiscretions regularly splashed across the tabloids.

Evan glanced to a balcony above the foyer, where guests mingled. He noted the guards blocking access to the hallways, and reasoned he'd have to devise a ploy to pass them to join the private party on the third floor. Thriving on challenges, Evan ascended the winding staircase, its intricately designed wrought iron rail twisting to the top. As he reached the landing, he smiled, scanning the scene for a patsy.

It took only seconds before selecting the perfect diversion. A thin blonde sipped a martini at the bar, engaged in a conversation with a twenty-something man whose muscles bulged through his two-sizes-too-small white T-shirt. The transparent material stretched tightly, his erect nipples and chest hair straining against the fabric. The beauty gave a pained smile as he slid his palm over her shoulder. His voice boomed throughout the room, and although he drew the occasional side eye from the crowd, no one intervened.

Evan inwardly laughed, giving a nod to a group of gorgeous women in the corner. No time for ladies tonight, he advanced toward his mark. He casually slipped his hand inside his pocket, sliding a finger into the hidden compartment. The size of a pencil eraser, the wisp of poisoned paper adhered to his finger. Initial testing of the organic prototype had proven successful in incapacitating an adult within fifteen seconds. Odorless, dissolvable on contact, the stamp was activated upon contact with blood, saliva, or sensitive mucous membranes such as the mouth or genitals, and of course, tonight's option, upon ingestion.

The short-lived results of one dose lasted exactly ten minutes. Victims never recalled the incident or the means of delivery, and no long-term effects had been observed. Heart rate and other vital signs remained intact yet no known antidote existed to revive the intended unconscious state. The wafer-thin weapon had been utilized in human trials, but the neophyte technology was only available to government agencies.

Evan eyed the man's cocktail as he set it on the bar, and increased his pace, advancing toward his target. His gait swayed as he pretended to be drunk.

"Pete. Pete...it's me, Patrick." Evan slurred his words as he stumbled toward the mark. Patrick had always been a favorite alias and slipped off his tongue as truth. As he lifted the stranger's drink, his finger dipped into the beverage, releasing the poison. Evan lifted it to his lips and continued. "It's been what? Three years since we ran the San Fran marathon. No, no...wait...was it two years ago?"

"What the hell, man? That's my drink there, asshole."

"Oh, yeah, sorry. My bad." Evan glanced to the glass and set it down gently, careful not to spill the liquid. He curled a finger at the bartender. "Hey, can I get a rum and Coke? I went to the john and someone jacked my drink. Can you believe that shit can happen at a shindig like this?"

"You sure you want another?" the muscle-bound stranger asked with a condescending tone.

"Two years, right? Geez, it was foggy that day. I could hardly see." Evan paused to accept his drink from the barkeep and took a sip. "I'm getting ready to run Boston this year but I usually stick to the West Coast."

"You've got the wrong guy. Look, I'm busy here." His eyes darted to the blonde, who nervously played with her hair. Evan wondered why the girl bothered staying, if she was entertaining the casting couch.

"Yeah, yeah. No worries. Have fun." Evan held up his glass and nodded, turning away. He gave a closed smile as he took a step toward the balcony railing. In his peripheral vision, he watched as the man gulped his drink. Evan eyed the guarded hallway and silently counted the seconds. *Ten. Nine. Eight. Seven. Six. Five. Four. Three. Two. One.*

The high-pitched scream echoed, drawing the attention of those guests on the second-floor landing. As guards and partygoers swarmed around the fallen body, Evan slipped away unnoticed. Quickly making his way down the hall to a side stairway, he bounded upward to investigate.

Evan remained in the shadows, traversing the hallway with stealthy precision as he attempted to avoid the detection of the overhead dome security cameras. All eyes would be on the victim, attempting to wake him. Vital signs would register normal. Evan expected guards would relocate the guest to a private location while they tried to wake him. They'd hesitate to call the police or paramedics, reluctant to disrupt the event. In exactly nine minutes, he'd wake and they'd send the drunken guest home in a cab.

Evan drew closer to the third floor, and the faint

whispers of an argument grew louder. As he approached the door, he recognized the female and stopped cold, listening.

"I thought you said you'd be able to help us get the data," the unfamiliar male voice growled.

"I told you that I worked there. I'll get you what you want, but it comes at a price," the female responded.

"Five million cash. It's what we're willing to pay. This is not news. Take it or leave it."

"And I told you, I don't just want money. I want names," she replied.

"Names?" he laughed. "Are you fucking kidding? These people are everyone and no one. Names will get you killed as soon as you blink."

"Names are part of the price," she demanded.

"You've got a death wish, lady. My contacts…there's no fucking way they want this shared with the likes of you. And now that Mr. Marretta and I have approached them, arranged for this exchange, we're all at risk. You're going to get us all killed."

"I don't give a shit what you think. Names are and have always been part of the deal."

"What kind of shit are you into? Blackmail?"

"I'm a collector of sorts. But for the sake of your boss, let's call it protection should any of these folks decide to come after me. If everyone plays nice, we have no issues. The clients get what they want. I disappear quietly. Everyone's happy. The terms of this deal are non-negotiable." She sighed, shook her head in disgust, and took off toward the door. "Look, if you can't make this happen,

I'm out of here. I want to speak with Mr. Marretta. I tire of
dealing with the B team."

Evan held his breath as the sound of her heels clicking
grew louder. He glanced to his watch. *Seven minutes.*

"Where the fuck do you think you're going?" the male
demanded.

"Get your fucking hand off of me right now, or neither
you nor Mr. Marretta will ever see me again," she promised,
her voice terse.

"I'm going to tell you what's going to happen right now.
There's a party going on downstairs."

"What are you saying?"

"I'm going to teach you a lesson in how Dom negotiates.
How I negotiate."

"I'm warning you right now," she told him, her voice
firm but calm, "get your fucking hands off me or you'll
regret it."

"You know what I want to know? Why did Dom let you
into our circle? Why does he trust you anyway? You're a
dumb bitch who just wasted our time. We already arranged
this deal and now you're fucking around. I've got news for
you. My time is expensive. And this pussy right here is
payment for my wasted time. I'm going to split you open,
little girl. Give you something to remember me by and then
you're going to get the data for me. You'll be thanking me
when I'm done."

"Do it," she challenged with a laugh.

Evan's heartbeat sped up at her words. What the ever-
loving fuck was she doing?

"Here's a bit of advice. Scream all you want. No one's going to hear you. I promise only to bruise you where they can't see. This time."

"Yeah, that's not gonna happen, asshole. How 'bout you scream for me?"

Evan heard the sound of flesh meeting flesh and tore into the room. Blood gushed from the large thug's nose as the female broke free of his hold and smacked him across the face with a glass statue. Her attacker rushed forward, shoving her into the wall, and without missing a beat she kneed him in the balls, driving him to the ground.

"Your mama didn't teach you any manners, did she?" she seethed, fire in her eyes.

"You're both dead," the male grunted, catching sight of Evan.

"We all gotta go sometime. But not today." Evan shrugged with a smile and landed a fist on his jaw. A loud thud sounded as the woman's assailant fell unconscious to the floor.

"Evan," the female whispered, her eyes wide on his.

"Raine."

"I've got this," she insisted. "You've got to go."

"Like hell you do. You're going to get us both killed. What the fuck do you think you're doing?"

Raine rolled her eyes and tugged down her white spandex dress. She reached for a matching pump that had fallen off her foot, slipped it on, and glanced around the room. "My purse."

"Forget your goddamned purse." Evan checked his watch. *Two minutes.*

"I've got it," Raine responded, lifting it up off the floor. "We've got to go now."

"Fine," she agreed, reluctance in her tone. "Come on. We can get out the back."

"Jesus, Raine. Just how the hell do you know this place so well?" Evan asked. He slid the backs of his knuckles across the emerald sofa, depositing a smear of blood onto its fabric, and poked his head around the doorjamb to check for guards. "It's clear but not for long. My car's parked a block away. Let's go."

"To the left," she instructed.

"Yeah, I've got it." It would only be a matter of seconds before someone saw the video of him in the room upstairs. Evan led them into the shadows toward a staircase farther down the hallway. "Goes to the kitchen, yes?"

"The caterers are in there but we should be able to slip out the alleyway. They'll be looking for us though. We are so fucked," she gritted out as they bounded down the flight of stairs.

As they reached the kitchen, Evan blocked her from going farther.

"What the hell are you doing?" she whispered.

"Hold up." He peeked into the room. Several cooks and waiters buzzed around the area, all focused on their work. Evan's eyes met Raine's. "Out the back door and to my car. Follow me. If they come for me, run as far as you can get on foot. I will come for you."

"I don't need saving."

"Sweetheart…" He gave a small smile, recalling how

she'd handled the guy upstairs. "After what I saw tonight, I'm tempted to agree, but you and I are as good as dead if we don't make ourselves scarce. Now."

Evan took her hand in his, shoving away the electricity that tingled in his palm. Tonight they'd have it out, and one way or another he'd find out what kind of shit she was into. For months he'd wanted to fuck his lovely coworker, but after overhearing her conversation, it was likely he'd kill her by his own hand or she'd be spending a long time in a government lockdown facility. A shame, really, but business was business.

As they tore into the kitchen, he dragged her, weaving through the sea of uniformed staff. A pan dropped, hitting the floor with a loud clang, and he looked over his shoulder, noting the five armed guards barreling toward them.

"Move," Evan told her. "Sorry, buddy." He snatched a silver tray out of a waiter's hands, and puff pastries flew into the air as he hurled it towards the barrage of goons who screamed at them to stop.

"This way." Raine pointed to the back exit.

Evan tugged a carving knife from a cook, shoving through the crowded kitchen. The swinging doors banged against the wall as he shouldered them open. A few cooks who stood smoking in the side alleyway made no move to stop them as they ran away.

"Keep going. They won't fire shots here at the house," Evan told her.

"Yeah, they'll find us later and kill us." Raine tore her hand from his as they broke into a sprint down the street.

"Here." Evan shoved his hand into his pocket and depressed the remote, unlocking the car.

"I'm not getting paid enough," Raine remarked at the sight of his expensive vehicle.

"Seems to me you're doing just fine with the money you're demanding." Evan didn't bother opening the door for the woman who had attempted to illegally sell data that didn't belong to her. "Get the fuck in."

"What crawled in your bed and died?" she asked, rolling her eyes. She opened her door, jumped in, and slammed it shut.

"Are you fucking for real, Raine?" Evan blew out a breath and shook his head, tossing the knife to the ground. He opened his door, slipped inside, and started the engine. "No, you know what? Don't say another fucking word. But you go ahead and think about what you're going to say."

"About what?" Raine's face tensed as she glanced in the side mirror. Headlights flashed in the distance. "We've got company."

"The truth. That's what the hell what." Evan shifted into gear and slammed his foot on the accelerator.

The wheels squealed, and the scent of burnt rubber permeated the car's interior. Evan wrenched the steering wheel to the right, taking the vehicle around a hairpin curve and down a side street. His eyes flashed to the rearview mirror, noting the lights behind him.

"Whatever shit you're into, you're in it deep. I want to know what shit. Whose shit. And how far you're swimmin' in it..." Evan paused as he raced into an underpass.

Switching lanes, he passed several cars until they emerged from the tunnel. He slammed on the brakes, sending the car spinning, and by the time they stopped, they were facing in the other direction. Spotting a dark alleyway, he sped into it and shut off the lights.

"Just because I didn't kill you back there for offering to sell government secrets," he continued, "that doesn't mean I won't. You have secrets, sweetheart, but so do I. My guess is that you aren't carryin', but be prepared because I'm searchin' your ass for weapons when we get to our destination."

"And where exactly is that?" Raine twisted to look out the back window. "That's them there. They passed. Jesus Christ, you're right about one thing, we're in some shit."

"Correction, sweetheart. You're in some shit. I'm not the one sellin' what doesn't belong to me."

"I would never do anything to hurt Emerson Industries or this country, and you fucking know it." Raine glanced to her blood-splattered dress and sighed. "Damn. I'm never gonna get that out. I just bought this. And I looked good in it too."

"You're cold, girl. I'll give you that." He shrugged and fired the engine up. "Tell you what. If I find you're telling the truth, that what you were doing was something other than what I thought it was, then I'll buy ya a new one. But I can promise you this. Lie to me? You're goin' to lose a lot more than an overpriced dress."

"It's not what you think," she protested.

"Just stop. You just sit there and work on your story. Later. I want the truth. All of it."

"But…"

"Not another word." Evan shifted hard, his thoughts racing as he tore down the I-5.

Raine Presley. What the hell was she doing tonight? Not for a minute would he have pegged her as a corporate spy. A fearless skydiver, Raine had joined Club Altura a year after starting her employment at Emerson Industries. As the chief security officer, she reported to Garrett on paper, but it was Evan who oversaw her work.

For months Evan had fought his attraction to her. Office dating wasn't an option. Not dipping his pen in the company ink had been a hard-and-fast rule that had served him well. A moment of pussy could be sweet as sugar but bitter as fuck the minute it turned. Although technically he wasn't her boss, the managerial lines blurred, and it could easily be argued he'd pressured her into it.

As the months progressed, their unsated sexual chemistry morphed into a heated, quick-witted banter that only served to fuel his desire for her. Despite the ongoing fantasy and temptation, logic warned him to stay away.

Evan had found it particularly difficult to resist her at Club Altura events. From skydiving to rock climbing, the members skirted the edge of death and openly explored their sexuality within the confines of Garrett Emerson's beachfront retreat. He found it interesting how the attractive executive would flirt yet never indulge in the more adventurous sexual activities. While Evan had publicly played with women, engaging in the occasional fling, he'd often catch her watching, a craving flickering in her hungry eyes.

He glanced to Raine who checked her phone. He noted the emerging bruises on her skin, a small trickle of dried blood on her shoulder. His mind churned as he recalled how she'd fought her attacker. He'd been in the military and had witnessed violence firsthand. She'd defended herself with an effortless precision and accuracy, which told him she'd been trained. The question was, by whom and for what purpose?

Evan focused on the road and sped toward San Diego. They'd have only hours to secure extra protection, decide next steps. Dom Marretta would want answers as to why he'd gone snooping at his party. Evan would claim he'd simply wandered in search of a restroom. As for Raine, he still couldn't be sure of the consequences of her actions. Once they arrived at his house, he'd either get the truth or, if not, he'd turn her over to the authorities himself.

∼⊰ Chapter Two ⊱∼

Raine stepped into the darkened foyer and released the breath she'd been holding for what seemed like forever. *Evan Tredioux. What the hell was he doing at the party tonight?* She'd been close to gathering the names of over a half dozen suspects, ones who sought to harm the country. Marretta's henchman had unexpectedly double-crossed her, refusing to give her the names she was promised in exchange for the data. As soon as he'd laid his fingers on her, she'd been set on taking him out, well before Evan made an appearance. She could have hidden her skills from him, but she'd chosen to defend herself first and then come up with a defensible lie.

Raine's father had been in the CIA, so she was no stranger to the life. Concerned that harm would come to his family, her daddy had trained her to kill when she'd been ten years old. Living in fear most of her childhood, Raine had deliberately chosen a different life, a safe one. She'd studied hard throughout school, landing herself a full scholarship to Harvard. Her mother had prayed she'd major in finance or law, land herself a rich husband. But Raine had decided long ago she wouldn't rely on anyone but herself. She'd majored in technology and secured a coveted internship at L-Tech. Within a year, she'd transferred over to Emerson Industries, quickly climbing the corporate ladder to lead their security team.

When Dom Marretta had approached her in a coffee shop, she'd immediately decided to take it to her contacts in the government. Ever since, she'd been a spy for a covert government organization. As she was deep undercover, neither Garrett nor Evan knew of her deception. It was true; she'd stolen bits of harmless information from Emerson Industries and delivered them to Marretta to show good faith. She'd systematically proved her worth to him, slowly earning his trust. But tonight he'd blown her off, instead choosing to delegate negotiation for payment to an underling.

As she reflected on the evening, she considered that if there was a bright side, it was that Dom would review the security footage and observe her taking out one of his best men. Although he'd be pissed that she'd insisted on the names, he'd always known it had been part of the deal, and she'd earn respect for her actions. Evan, however, was a complication. She'd have only hours to figure out how to explain his presence.

With spies everywhere, Marretta would find them eventually. Before that happened, she'd have to get the hell out of wherever Evan had taken her and go back to the event on her own. She'd save face by doing so, but if he suspected she'd told Evan about their criminal activities, he'd swiftly order both their deaths. Raine would play it off as keeping with her cover. She'd tell him that she'd been as surprised as anyone to see Evan and had decided to go with him to distract him from the deal, draw attention away from the gala.

As Raine ran through a litany of plausible lies in her mind, a door slammed behind her, causing her to startle. *Evan.* He'd press her for answers. She'd have to tell him just enough to satisfy him without divulging everything, exposing her mission.

"Whatever you're thinking, it better be good," he commented.

"I'm not thinking anything," she lied.

Her anxiety rose as Evan pecked a code into a pad on the wall, activating the home's security system. There was no way she'd escape without him knowing. She'd been trained in fighting, not disabling alarms.

"I don't know what's going on, Raine, but I want answers starting now," he told her and switched on the lights.

"But I…" She lost her words as Evan stripped off his shirt, revealing his tanned, corded muscles. With his back turned, he waved a hand at her to follow him.

She struggled to concentrate, a rush of desire threading through her body. For as long as she could remember, she'd fantasized about making love with Evan. Chills danced over her skin as she recalled the last time they'd worked on a joint presentation, the delicious scent of his cologne enticing her senses as he'd peered over her shoulder.

Despite the opportunity to act on sexual impulses at Club Altura parties, Raine had been hesitant to engage in the activities. Her attraction to Evan had been unrivaled by any other man. He was the only one she'd ever wanted. She suspected if she slept with him, it was likely she'd want him forever. Pursuing him would only lead to heartbreak. If by some miracle Garrett didn't fire her when the mission was all over, it wasn't likely Evan would ever look at her the same way again.

Raine had seen him with women at the lavish events and often retreated. She loathed the jealousy that curled in her chest, but she'd been careful not to show it, afraid to damage their relationship. Logic told Raine to forget him, but the fantasy of being in his arms and bed lingered.

"Raine," she heard him call to her, breaking her contemplation. He spun around, pinning her with his penetrating blue eyes. Her heart pounded in her chest as he stalked toward her.

"I'm sorry. I...I..." She averted her gaze, afraid she'd confess how she felt. Raine glanced to her arm and sighed at the sight of the dried blood. In her adrenaline-fueled escape, she hadn't noticed the scratch.

"Are you sure you're okay?" he asked, his voice softening as he approached.

"I...uh, yeah, I'm fine." A myriad of emotions twisted through her as he drew closer. Relief she'd survived. Fear he'd grow angry. Arousal.

"Raine..."

As he closed the distance, she stepped backward, her

shoulders brushing the wall. She licked her lips as he pressed into her.

"I've known you for what? Five years now, maybe?" he asked.

"Four." Raine's green eyes drifted up to meet his. He towered above her, the heat of his body emanating onto her skin. "What are you doing?"

"There hasn't been one project where I haven't been able to rely on you to hit a home run. Everything we've done has been successful. There isn't one jump we've done where I wouldn't have trusted you to pull my cord. And then tonight…"

"It's not what you think… I can explain."

"Tell me I didn't hear what I heard tonight."

She closed her eyes, releasing a breath as he flattened his palms on the wall, caging her with his arms.

"Selling data? Demanding names? Why does someone do these things? Stealing. What the hell were you doing?"

"I…" Her lids lifted, her gaze slowly meeting his. She'd craved him since the first time they'd worked together, and now he thought her a liar, a thief. This was never her intention when she'd agreed to help the agency. "It's complicated."

"I bet it is. But you'd better fucking tell me right now or I'm calling the police. Don't even fuck with me, because I'll know if you're lying."

"I told you. It's not what you think. You know me," she insisted. It wasn't as if she didn't get why he thought she'd betrayed him, Emerson Industries, and the country. Raine's chest tightened as her words danced on the tip of her tongue. "I'd never sell our secrets to someone like Dom Marretta. I can't tell you what I'm doing but you have to trust me."

"Who?" he asked with a raised eyebrow.

"What?" she stammered. Her heart pounded as Evan leaned in close, his eyes locked on hers.

"Who do you work for?"

"You know who I work for. Emerson Industries. The same place you do."

"What you did tonight…taking out that asshole. That wasn't the kind of guy just anyone can take on. You've been trained. So again, sweetheart, who?"

"I… Evan…please, I can't tell you but I swear to God I didn't…" Raine closed her eyes and sighed, as his warm breath teased her ear. Desire twisted through her body and she lost concentration. *Tell him anything he wants to know.* For so long, she'd denied herself pleasure. "I…I work for our government. I can't tell you who. I need the names of those guys they were selling the data to. That's all I can say, but you have to believe me. What you saw tonight, it's not what you think."

"Ah, a truth. Finally. Do you see how easy it can be? But still, my little thief, I want to know who. Who in the government do you work for? And what in the hell are these terrorists going to do with the data? Why would the government allow you to give it to them?"

"I can't tell you that. Jesus, Evan. You were in the military. You know I can't say." Her heart pounded in her chest. So close, her hands reached toward him, her palms pressed against his chest as his lips grazed her ear. "I swear to you though. The data was scrubbed. Please."

"Why don't you ever play at Club Altura?"

"What?" Raine stammered, shocked at the change of subject.

"The entire time you've belonged. I've never once seen you with anyone. Not even once."

Raine froze as he moved to tilt his head toward hers, his eyes on hers.

"Why is that?"

"I...I... It's just I've never wanted to..."

"I've seen the heat in your eyes. You want to, all right," he pressed.

"Why are you asking about this? I need to make a phone call and then get back to the party," she insisted, attempting to deny her body's response to him.

"Because, I know what you want, Raine," he said, his voice low. "I've always known."

"Please let me go. Dom wants the info I have. I need the names. I have to do something right now. Don't you understand how close I am to getting those names?" Anger flared in her eyes, yet as he inched closer, arousal flooded her body. "Evan..."

"The club. Not everyone plays openly. But you? Never. Not once."

"I don't want to talk about this." She pushed on his chest but he didn't budge.

"I do. Why? I want the truth."

"Why don't you ever choose me?" she countered, surprised at her response. As the words left her lips, she was helpless to stop them. "So many late nights. We've been working together forever. You never ask me… Not once did you… I just thought that maybe…"

"Maybe what?"

"That you…me…" She couldn't bring herself to articulate her fantasies.

"Say it, sweetheart. That what?" He gave a devious smile.

"Please," she sighed, closing her eyes. Raine's body prickled in awareness as he brought his lips to her ear once again.

"I've wanted you," he whispered. "So many nights."

"No," she responded, shock in her voice. "You never…"

"Because we work together. But at the club, you never play."

"Maybe that's because the one person I want to play with…I can't…" she breathed.

"Tell me what you want. Tell me, the truth."

Raine shuddered as his lips brushed her neck, and she found herself unable to keep her thoughts at bay. "I've always wanted…you…but you never…"

"I don't mess with people who report to me. But don't ever think I didn't want you," he told her.

"But…you…" Gooseflesh broke over her skin as he peppered kisses along her neck.

"You're fired." As Evan's lips crushed onto hers, Raine melted into his arms. His tongue swept into her mouth and she kissed him back with an urgent fervor. She shivered as his palms glided over her shoulders, trailing over her sensitive neck, sending tendrils of desire through her body. With a deliberate sensual control, his palms cupped her cheeks, deepening their kiss, his lips making love to hers.

Evan tore his lips from Raine's, his forehead pressed to hers. "I don't get involved with people who work for me."

"I…I can't promise when this is over I'll still be here." As her senses returned, logic warred with her arousal. After tonight, it'd be unlikely she'd still be in San Diego, let alone working for Emerson Industries.

"One night, Raine. Right now, I'm going with my gut here, trusting that you wouldn't steal. Whatever the hell you've got yourself into, I can't even think of letting you back in the doors of Emerson. Not until I know everything. Not until someone in the CIA, FBI, or NSA comes to me. Hell, after what just went down back there—"

"I've already got what I need," she confessed. The agency had given her dummy files to pawn off to Marretta in exchange for names. They were a mishmash of scrubbed data, with tidbits of fake information she'd created.

"One night," he repeated.

"One night." She nodded, taking a deep breath as her heart fluttered. *I'm going to regret this.*

She'd lied, all right. If she made love to him, once would never be enough. She'd always known that. After years of working and skydiving together, their relationship meant more to her than she'd admit. She'd never thought it possible to fall in love with someone she'd never kissed, yet when his lips had met hers, her heart crushed, confirming her suspicion. Her feelings ran deep, and there was no way she'd be able to stop the rush of emotion that had been kept at bay. Still, she willingly dove down the rabbit hole, praying she would survive.

Evan lifted her off the ground and cradled her to his chest. Raine wrapped her hands around his neck, molding her body to his, engulfed in his warmth. She closed her eyes, her mind churning as he carried her. Maybe the agency would vouch for her. Maybe he'd trust her again. Maybe she could stay in San Diego. Maybe he'd choose her and her only. *Maybe…*

The patter of water droplets broke her contemplation, and she blinked open her eyes. Her hands clutched his shoulders as he set her on her feet. She reached to remove her dress, and his firm voice stopped her cold.

"Raine."

"Yes," she whispered, her hands trembling.

"Don't move." He hooked his fingers around the thin spaghetti straps of her dress, dragging them over her shoulders. He never took his eyes off of hers as he tugged the fabric off her body, allowing it to pool on the floor. "Do you have any idea how long I've waited for you?"

"No…" Raine's heart skipped a beat as Evan spoke. Every single day, working side by side, the anguish of pretending she didn't want him had nearly killed her. But it had been nothing compared to watching him with other women, denying herself his affection, silently swallowing her jealousy.

"Our late nights." He gave a sexy smile and set his palms on her hips.

"I wanted to…"

"Jesus, you're gorgeous…always have been, but it's your mind that has always drawn me to you."

She gave a flirtatious smile, recalling their incessant banter. "Well, what can I say, sir? I can't let the boss think he knows everything."

Raine knew he was dominant. She'd watched him at Club Altura, taking control of his flavor of the month. While she'd never been submissive in the least in the office, regularly challenging him in the boardroom, the rush of jumping out of a plane at thirty-five thousand was nothing, she imagined, to the sting of his hand on her bottom.

"You've got quite a mouth on you, sweetheart."

Raine sucked in a breath as he reached for her hips and yanked her toward him, rocking his erection into her pelvis.

"This is just the beginning. That little mouth…" He dragged his thumb over her lower lip. "Let's see what you can do with it."

"What are you doing?" she gasped as he lifted her by the waist and set her into the warm spray.

Her heart pounded against her ribs as she watched him strip off his pants, his enormous cock springing forth. Evan kicked them off and stalked toward her. She breathed in anticipation as he closed the distance.

Raine sighed as his lips smashed onto hers, her body coming alive at his devastating kiss. His tongue swept into her mouth, tasting, probing. As he broke contact, she protested. "No…" Breathless, her body quivered in his arms.

"That little mouth of yours...I know exactly what I want to do with it," he told her, commanding her attention. He brushed his finger under her chin. "On your knees."

"What?" The shower mist clung to her lashes as she blinked up to meet his gaze.

"On your knees."

Shock rolled through her at his demand, but her pussy tightened in response, flooding in arousal. Raine had never considered doing anything like this for anyone, submitting. In the office, she'd just as soon tell him to go fuck himself. But in the shower, nude and vulnerable, her traitorous body reveled in his command.

"Did you hear me, little one? You've been enough trouble for tonight. Now, on. Your. Knees."

Raine shivered, his voice washing over her strong and clear. She did as she was told, her palms curling around the backs of his thighs as she knelt on the floor. With a heated gaze, she licked the moisture from her lips, waiting for his instruction.

"I've wanted you for the longest time. Now you're going to show me what you can do with that wicked little mouth of yours."

She reached for his cock, but he reprimanded her.

"Ah, ah, ah. No touching. Just open your lips, the ones that enjoy back talking me." He stroked himself as if baiting her to disobey.

Raine trembled, her mouth widening. As he dragged the thick head of his cock along her lower lip, her tongue darted over his wet slit, tasting his salty essence. Her pussy contracted, an ache throbbing between her legs.

"You've wanted this for so long and so have I. Tonight…" He inched his shaft inside her warmth. Raine moaned, sucking him as he slid his cock inside her mouth. "I'm going to make love to you all night. You'll never doubt that I've always wanted you."

Raine's heart caught on hearing his words. So much more between them than just lust. He'd known it, too, and whatever happened after they made love, she was certain they'd forever be connected.

"Fuck," he sighed, sliding himself in and out of her mouth.

She tightened her lips around his shaft, sucking hard while resisting the temptation to take him in her hands. Increasing her speed, she swallowed his hard length until he groaned.

"Aw, no…not coming in your mouth," he insisted.

She ignored him, lapping at his cock. A firm grasp into her wet hair, the sting to her scalp warned her to obey. As he tilted her head backwards, she released him with an audible pop, licking her lips. Inwardly she laughed, aware that it was she who still remained in control, but didn't dare speak a word.

She squealed as he reached under her arms and pulled her to her feet. His mouth slammed on hers, his devilish tongue sweeping against hers. Sucking and tasting, he demanded her presence, and Raine reveled in his control.

"Ah," Raine moaned into his touch. As he palmed her pussy, the tip of his finger feathered over her clit.

"How long have you wanted it? To make love? All those nights at Club Altura? The office?"

"Oh, yes," she breathed into his kiss. She dug her fingernails into his shoulders as he shoved a thick digit into her core, stretching her open.

"How long have you waited to be fucked?" he growled into her ear, taking the lobe between his teeth.

"So long. So fucking long," she responded.

"You're all mine tonight." Evan moved his lips to her chin and nipped at her lower lip. "This mouth." As he palmed her ass and teased his finger over her back hole, she shivered in his grip. "This too. You ever been fucked here, Raine? Because tonight this is mine too."

"I…I…I've never…"

"Do you want me to fuck your ass?"

"I…I…" She rested the back of her head on the tiles as he bit at her neck. She'd never talked dirty to another man, but her body responded, his crass language further driving the passion between them. He increased the pace, fucking her pussy with his hand.

"Hmm…let me see how tight you are."

Raine sucked in a breath as the tip of his finger probed her back hole. The dark fantasies she'd always harbored rushed to the forefront of her mind and her pussy contracted around his fingers, pulsating to the sensation.

"That's it, sweetheart. Jesus, I need to be in you."

As he stroked her clit, his fingers filling her, she succumbed to his pleasure. The overwhelming desire to confess her emotions stirred, but she reined it back, simply allowing her senses to fill her mind. Pleasure. Desire. Lust. Evan Tredioux was a cliff she'd willingly base jump off, and as she fell, she'd embrace the complete lack of control.

"You see, I've always had this talent for reading you," he continued, fucking her with his fingers, his lips on her neck. "All those late nights. The body responds in ways you don't notice. Your breath, the way you stretched your neck when I'd come close to you. The hunger in your eyes, watching me at the club."

"Oh, God." *Jesus, he knows.* She was so close to coming, and her embarrassment faded as he flicked the pad of his thumb over her clit.

"That's right, sweetheart. I saw you. Do you know it took fucking everything I had not to play with you? To pretend I didn't want you? But this…"

"Please don't stop," she cried.

"This tells me everything."

"I…I…" Raine panted as her body shook, the climax rocking through her. Exposed, she'd own the truth of wanting him, desiring him. He'd peel away the layers and reveal her true thoughts.

"But tonight you lied so I'm going to give you a little pain with that pleasure."

"No, no, no," she pleaded as he removed his fingers from her pussy and ass. Empty, she trembled as the tendrils of her orgasm rolled through her. As he turned her around, bent her forward, placing her hands on the wall, she continued to beg. "Don't stop. What are you doing?"

"I promise, Raine. If you know nothing else, know that

I will take care of you. Stay right here. Let me get a condom."

"I'm on the pill. Clean," she said, breathless.

"You sure about this?" he asked.

"Yes. Please…just…I can't wait."

"Trust?"

"I'm sure. Please…just don't stop," she pleaded.

"All right then. Let me see that beautiful ass of yours." He smiled, pleased as she bent over and spread her legs wide, her hands flattened against the wall. She wiggled her bottom at him, and he continued his instruction. "You like this, do you? I want to hear it then. Ask me to fuck you…nicely."

"Um…what?" she stammered.

"You heard me. Ask me." His fingers glided down her back, stroking her skin.

"No…I can't…"

"Now, Raine," Evan demanded.

"Ow…ah," she cried as he slapped her wet ass, the delicious pain sending a spear of erotic pleasure to her pussy. *Oh, my God. He knows everything. He knows what I've watched him do, what I want.*

"Stop thinking. Just let go," Evan told her, and another firm slap to her bottom sounded. "You've wanted this. I've wanted this. And now…we are finally together."

"Fuck me…ah yes" she breathed as the broad crown of his dick pressed into her core, stretching her. She widened her stance, accepting him, allowing him to slide deep inside her pussy. As she bent over, water dripped down her hair into her face. Her lips drenched, her tongue darted over the moisture.

"Raine..." he began but lost his words as he withdrew and slowly pressed back inside her.

"Yes...please, Evan," she pleaded.

Raine braced her hands onto the tiles and grunted as he slammed inside her. Her body tightened with desire with each hard thrust. She wiggled toward him, attempting to get him to go faster, but he continued his restraint. Evan twisted his palm into her wet locks and tugged, reminding her of his control. Her lips parted with a smile as his fingers gripped her shoulder and he slid inside her once again.

"You're so fucking tight. Fuck..." he grunted.

"That's it, yeah." Her core fisted his cock as he pounded into her. She gave a ragged breath with each delicious stroke.

As he released her hair, her head lolled forward. His fingers teased down her spine. "This, though."

Raine's heart pounded in anticipation as his thumb trailed down the crevice of her ass. She startled in response to his touch. As he teased her puckered hole with his slippery finger, another layer played to her arousal.

"Do it. Please...ah, yes." The dark pleasure blossomed, and she found herself begging.

"Easy, now...ah yeah." Evan slowed his pace.

"Ev...Evan," she panted as the tip of his thumb penetrated her ass, a twinge of pain radiating through the tight ring of muscle. Slowly, he pressed inside until he'd filled her completely.

"That's a girl. See how good that is." He gently worked the ring of muscle until she relaxed into his touch.

"Yes, oh God...don't stop."

Slowly he rocked inside her, gradually increasing the pace.

"I…I… please…" Raine lost focus as his fingers slid through her slick folds, teasing her swollen nub. With his thumb inside her ass, and his other hand playing at her clit, she sucked in a breath. So full and overwhelmed with sensation, she tilted her hips, moaning as her climax teetered on the edge. As he withdrew his cock and thrust inside her, a rush of fresh arousal surfaced, hurling her toward her orgasm.

"Aw fuck, Raine. You feel so good," he praised, pressing his thumb into her back hole in tandem as he fucked her.

"Please…please…do it…like that. Ah, yeah…it feels so good." His fingers danced over her clitoris, increasing the pressure. As he rocked into her pussy, Raine's body shook, the wave of ecstasy claiming her. She screamed his name as her orgasm rocked through her, holding firmly to the wall as Evan gave a final thrust, his grunt echoing in the shower.

Raine went limp, releasing a sigh. As he removed himself and gently lifted her into his arms, her chest tightened in emotion, a hot tear running down her cheek. Never in her life had she let a man speak the way he had to her, fuck her the way he'd done, and her heart crushed, aware she'd beg him to do it again. She wanted Evan in her life, and not just for a night. Her mind raced at the thought of losing him, barely noticing as he laid her on the bed.

Raine curled away from Evan as he pressed his lips to the back of her wet hair. A warm towel draped over her body, and she attempted to shove her feelings away. *You'll never*

have Evan, a voice in her head told her. *Fuck him. Enjoy it.
Then get back to work.* He was a player. And she was a spy.
Some things, no matter how much you wanted them,
weren't meant to be.

⤚❦ *Chapter Three* ❦⤚

The second he'd kissed her, he knew he shouldn't make love to her. Every late night. Every inside joke. The sexual tension that had built over four years wouldn't be sated in one night.

Fucking feelings. Jesus Christ. The moment her soft lips touched his, it confirmed his worst fear. He'd seen the way she'd watched him at the club, knew the moment he pushed her, she'd willingly submit. She'd come undone under his touch. He'd deliberately fucked her from behind, avoiding the surge of emotion he suspected he'd feel if he looked into her eyes.

He'd pulled his dick out and lifted Raine into his arms without saying a word. Although she attempted to shield her face, the tears trailing her cheeks told him that their relationship had transformed forever. She'd play it off as nothing but he knew their one-time friendship had been permanently replaced by a ravenous craving that wouldn't be satisfied by a one-night stand.

Evan set her gently on the bed and returned to the

bathroom to turn off the water. He glanced in the mirror and shook his head. Guilt teemed through him, as he was aware he'd crossed a line. *Jesus fucking Christ, you're an idiot.* What if she was lying? Although his gut told him she was telling the truth, doubt crept inside his mind.

He shook off the thought and returned with a towel. As Evan approached, he smiled, finding her curled onto her side. His little badass spy had fought a three-hundred-pound thug but now hid from him. It wasn't as if the intimacy hadn't grabbed him by the balls, but if he'd learned anything in his lifetime, you had to man up and face your fears.

"Hey." Her reddened eyes flashed up to him and she gave a small smile. Gently grazing the towel over her skin, Evan spoke as he dried her. "You all right?"

"Yeah, I'm fine," she replied, her voice shaken.

"Raine."

"Yeah?"

"You're beautiful. Tonight, it was amazing."

"It was unbelievable. I've never felt like that before," she confessed.

"Come here." Evan tossed the towel aside and lay onto his back. Sliding his arm underneath her, he cradled her to his chest. He stared up at the full moon through the ceiling skylights and sighed. "Tell me what you're thinking."

"I'm thinking...I don't know..." She hesitated.

"It's okay to be honest. We worked together all this time. Jumped too. Trust. It's something we always had. I have to believe whatever you're doing, you wouldn't do it without giving it serious consideration. I've never seen you do anything without carefully weighing the consequences."

"It's just...I've only dated one other person from Emerson."

Evan knew she'd dated his friend, Chase Abbott, well before she'd ever taken over as Emerson's chief security officer. But he had insisted they were nothing more than friends and had gone as far as to encourage Evan to ask her on a date.

"Chase and I. It was never serious. We're just friends. We definitely didn't play openly at Club Altura. I'm not like that. Or at least...I don't know. Maybe I am. Maybe you were the only one I wanted to play with."

"But you wanted this tonight. Us."

"For the longest time," she confessed, raising her eyes to meet his. Raine sighed and laid her cheek back onto his chest. "What we just did... God, it was amazing. But you know I'd never be the one to initiate. And you..."

"You knew I didn't date people at the office."

"Yeah. People talk. And frankly, as much as I wanted this, to be together, I didn't want to risk my job. I love working at Emerson. When this thing with Dom came along...I didn't ask for it to happen. But I couldn't ignore the opportunity to take him down either, to go after a few bad guys. My Dad was in the CIA. I may not have wanted a life of danger, but I'm not a coward. I love my country. So after I got involved with the Feds, I had to finish what I started."

"Yeah." Evan couldn't commit to understanding a

situation without having all the facts. Until she divulged everything, he couldn't comment further. Saying he trusted her was as far as he could go.

"You don't believe me." Her voice faltered in disappointment.

"I want evidence. I want to know the name of the organization. I want to talk to them."

"All I can promise is that I'll ask them. You were in the military. These things…involvement with the Feds…I can't just go breaking protocol no matter how much I want to tell you." Raine pushed up on his chest and looked him directly in his eyes. "When this is over, I'll tell you one way or another. I promise you. I swear to God I'm not lying."

"Didn't you ever want to play at Club Altura?" Evan changed the subject, determined to peel away her layers.

"Truth?"

"Yeah. Truth."

"I don't know. It's not like I'm a prude. It's just that, I don't know. I just started going to the events a few years ago. I was working with you. And I just had this idea…that you and I, we'd had this connection. So it just felt like if I did that, if I had sex with someone else, like maybe that would say something to you."

"I had sex with other people. You watched." Evan detected the flash of pain in her eyes but she quickly recovered, forcing an impassive expression.

"You chose to do that."

"They weren't members of the club."

"Why did you do it? If you wanted me, was it a message?"

"Not deliberate. But you?"

Raine sighed, trailing her finger over his chest. "I've wanted you forever. But we couldn't... You never attempted to kiss me or anything. And then I saw you with the women. And I don't know. I questioned if that's something I want. Not everyone does those things. If I was going to do it...it would only be with you. No one else."

"What I did, you know it wasn't serious. I'm not seeing anyone. You know how it is there," Evan attempted to explain. He'd never given a thought to what he was doing at Club Altura as long as it wasn't with an employee.

"Things just got to a point where I knew..." She blew out a breath and hesitated.

"Knew what?"

"I'd want more. One night. I get that's what we said, but Evan...I don't want to be a one-night stand. I don't want this to be the end of us," she confessed.

"It doesn't have to be." Evan weighed his next words, careful not to make empty promises. "If Marretta doesn't kill us both, and the Feds you're working for spill the truth, then we can see what happens. Whoever it is you work for, these assholes should have come to Garrett and me instead of you. I'm not going to bother asking you any more about the situation, because I get they'll come down on you, but tomorrow, Garrett and I will find out who it is, and the shit will hit the fan. It's not like we haven't cooperated in the past. This is some bullshit. They put all of us in danger."

"Marretta's going to try to kill you." Her voice fell to a whisper. "You don't know him. I've seen things." She shivered in his arms, calming as he ran his hand down her shoulder. "He's a monster."

"I'm not letting you go back to him. I don't give a shit what agency you're working for. It's too dangerous." Evan released an even breath, attempting to conceal his anger.

"I don't have a choice." She sighed. "Besides, I'm close to getting this done, getting names. Dom will respect me for what I did. He'll question why I went with you, but I'll lie. He'll buy it. I'll get the damn names. They'll get some shitty dummy file. By the time they run the data, double- and triple-check, I'll be out of there. You should know, though, if I don't leave here soon, the Feds will come for me. You'll be charged with holding me. They'll make up something. There are dark recesses of our government. Invisible agencies. They report to few and do what they want. They don't even register with most senators or representatives. No one knows about them."

Evan considered her words. It was true that there were ultra-secret operations, spy agencies that never surfaced, let alone went public. They'd sooner make her disappear from the face of the earth than allow her to refuse to complete the mission.

"I'll go with you," he said.

"I can't put you in danger," she replied.

"I may not be able to control what's going on tonight, but Garrett and I, between the two of us, we can rein this situation in, find out the organizations that are driving this effort and get you out."

"Do you have any weapons here?" She glanced around

his bedroom and smiled. "Wherever here is?"

"More than you'd know what to do with, sweetheart."

"All right then. We'll play it your way but you have to stay far behind. If they see you, we're both dead."

"You'll deny that you knew I was following you."

"I can do that but he'd probably kill us. They'd definitely kill you, Evan. I can't let that happen." Panic laced her voice.

"I know what I'm doin'. Not my first time at the rodeo. I'll be invisible."

"We've got to get out soon. I have a few contacts of my own who expect me to report. And if the Feds show up, it's not going to be a good situation. We're going to be fucked. I need to get back on the job. I'll get the names and get out." Raine shoved up onto her elbows, attempting to leave.

"Not so fast, sweetheart." Evan rolled Raine onto her back, and she squealed in laughter as he pinned her arms to the bed. He settled between her legs, his cock lengthening as she arched her back, her breasts brushing his chest.

"Hmm…I like you this way."

"Vulnerable?" she asked.

"With me. That's how."

A broad smile crossed her face. "Me too."

"We've always made a good team, you know that?"

"The best. No one could mess with us in the boardroom."

"We'd make a better team now."

"Are you saying you'd like to change the terms of this agreement?" She raised an eyebrow, giving him a sexy smile.

"I'm thinking…" He laughed. "Yeah, I'd like to renegotiate."

"I'm open to hearing your proposal, Mr. Tredioux."

"After this mess is cleaned up, I want a proper date." Evan's lips moved to her neck, tasting her delicate skin.

"Yes," she laughed.

"But you can't work for me. I was serious about the being fired part."

"Hmm...that much I expected. Ah..." She wriggled underneath him, rocking her pelvis against his thickening cock.

"If you're telling the truth, I'll go to bat for you with Garrett. If not, no dinner date."

"I'm not lying. Besides, who said dinner was our date?" she countered.

Evan laughed. Although she was gorgeous, her wit was something he'd always found particularly attractive. "Rock climbing. Then dinner. No arguing. Dinner is always required for a date."

"What girl can resist rock climbing? Ahh..." she moaned as he peppered kisses down her breast, a nipple slipping between his lips. "Evan..."

"You're beautiful," he murmured, his mouth full.

"Please..."

"I want to taste every inch of you," he told her as he released her swollen tip.

With his cock painfully hard as steel, he resisted shoving himself inside her. Slowly, he nipped and sucked at her abdomen, shifting himself downward, between her legs.

"That's a girl. Let me see that beautiful pussy of yours." He trailed his lips over her mound and spread her labia open with his thumbs.

"Evan," she cried as he stroked his tongue through her slick folds.

He lapped at her clit, tasting her sweet essence on his lips. Lifting her bottom with one hand, he speared his tongue into her core. While flicking her swollen bead with his thumb, he fucked her pussy. She bucked wildly, but he held firm, his fingers gripping her ass. Raine screamed his name, and her head thrashed as her entire body quivered, her hands gripping the sheets as he relentlessly milked her orgasm.

As her cries faltered, he rose above her, settling his cock between her legs. He licked his lips, his hunger flaring in his eyes. With a deliberate motion, he stroked the tip of his hard length through her slick folds, teasing her clit.

Emotion rose in his chest as he gazed into her eyes. He prayed like hell she was telling the truth, that every shred of intuition that told him she was innocent was on point. He shoved the thoughts to the back of his mind as she mewled, and glided his palms over her full breasts. Slowly, inch by inch, Evan eased his cock into her tight core. Raine opened to him, her knees falling to the sides, moaning as he filled her completely.

As he rested on his forearms, his fingers tunneled into her silken locks. He kissed her with passion, releasing the emotion he couldn't articulate. A master of restraint, Evan finally let go, making love to Raine. Her magical kiss weaved a spell, and in that moment, he knew he'd fight to keep her in San Diego.

As he increased his pace, thrusting inside her, she tilted

her hips to meet his. She wrapped her legs around his waist, drawing him deeper. With his forehead to hers, their heated gazes silently communicated the feelings neither would dare speak. His breath quickened as he drew closer to orgasm, his pelvis grazing her clit.

"Evan...oh, God. I...I..." Raine panted.

"Fuck...yes..." Evan grunted, unable to control the climax that rocked through him. His seed exploded deep inside Raine as her core quivered around his cock. Waves of ecstasy rippled through him, and his lips smashed onto hers, muffling her screams of pleasure. He gave a final thrust before gently slipping out of her and rolling to his back, keeping her close to his chest.

"Raine, I need you to know—"

"I don't want this to end," she interrupted, her breath ragged.

"Nothing will happen to you," he promised, inwardly cursing the situation.

Evan held her tightly, swearing he'd keep her alive. He'd decided to call on his good friend Dean Frye, who was an assistant district attorney. They'd have to work fast. The longer she took to get back to Dom Marretta and give him the data, the more likely it was he'd doubt her story.

Exhausted, Evan closed his eyes and pressed his lips to her hair. As she fell asleep in his arms, he considered the array of weapons stocked in his home. Garrett joked he was paranoid, but Evan preferred to think of his enthusiasm as actively prepared.

He smiled as her lips touched his chest, reminding him of the secrets that lay in his heart. His lioness would fight to the death. He'd seen her in action and had no doubt she'd push the limits to get the names. But no matter her confidence that Dom would believe her, that she'd be safe, Evan couldn't take that risk and let her go it alone.

Raine imagined a life without espionage or danger. When she'd agreed to the mission, the element of death had seemed worth the risk. But within Evan's embrace, she questioned everything; her career, her decisions, her life.

As he'd made love to her, she could feel every thread of his emotion. The connection they'd built over time, as friends…now lovers, was stronger than ever. Nothing would ever be the same.

Her heart constricted as she snuggled against his chest, attempting to memorize the exact way it felt. His masculine scent. The strength of his arms. The pace of his breathing as his chest rose and fell, the rough pad of his fingers trailing over her arm.

Evan had always represented power and intelligence, a charismatic rainmaker. The man who'd haunted her dreams had finally become reality. After tasting his passion, she refused to give him up without a fight. She'd go to Dom tonight, give him the data, and complete her mission. But if he so much as laid a finger on Evan, she'd shoot him dead without blinking an eye. Evan was hers and no one, not a mob boss, not the government, would take him away.

As sleep claimed her, dreams of rock climbing danced in her head. A summit. Dinner for two. A kiss. *Evan Tredioux.*

❧ *Epilogue* ❧

As Raine pulled away in the cab, Evan switched on the ignition of his car. He'd called in a favor with Dean and arranged to have an undercover cop drive her to Marretta's mansion. Although the police were on alert, they'd been cautioned not to interfere with the covert action.

Raine had already texted Marretta, alerting him that she'd arrive within a few hours. She'd fed him a lie about Evan accidentally finding her upstairs, that he'd insisted she leave the party and she'd only gone along with him so he wouldn't cause a scene. She'd claimed Evan had taken her to a diner in San Clemente, where he'd interrogated her for hours over coffee but eventually bought her story. Marretta had insisted the deal was still on and agreed to give her the names and money. Although he'd appeared satisfied with Raine's explanation of the night's events, Evan's intuition told him something was wrong. With the way they'd torn out of his house, there was no way Marretta would let her off the hook so easily. But Raine insisted that she knew Marretta better than he did. With the Feds minutes away,

Evan had no choice but to let her go about her mission.

In the obscurity of the night on the I-5, Evan had lost a visual on her cab nearly ten minutes ago. The police vehicle, disguised as a taxi, had been outfitted with a tracking device. Evan had deliberately kept far behind, remaining invisible in case Marretta had eyes on the cab. He glanced at the blip on his cell phone as it inched toward LA, his stomach dropping when, in an instant, the car disappeared from his screen.

As he tapped at the glass, praying it was a malfunction, a loud horn sounded behind him. The tractor trailer had come up from behind in darkness, and he knew he was in trouble. The flare of its headlights glared into his rear window, blinding him as he sped to avoid the impact. The crunch of metal scraping metal sounded, and as the car spun off the highway, he wrestled with the wheel. Darkness claimed its victim, and the only thought in his head was Raine.

"What did she say? Fucking tell me now." The deafening command rang in his ears.

"I'm going to kill you," Evan promised, his naked body slumped forward, blood pooling in his mouth. He'd been in and out of consciousness for hours. Tied to a bar on the ceiling, he forced his mind into survival mode, resorting to his military training.

"What's your relationship?" his captor barked. Landing

a solid blow to Evan's ribs, he laughed as crimson body fluid splattered onto the floor.

"Fuck you," Evan grunted, breathless from the impact.

"What did Raine tell you?" His attacker spun, punching him hard across his jaw.

Evan's vision blurred, the jolt of pain spearing through him. He blinked, taking in his surroundings, spying his weapon of choice.

"I'm going to kill you," Evan spat again, formulating his plan. Dean and his buddies were waiting for a text from him. When it didn't come, they'd rain hell down upon Dom Marretta and his henchmen. The tracker would provide evidence as to where Raine was delivered.

"Wrong, buddy," the stranger laughed. "You're not going anywhere. You're already dead. You just don't know it."

"I'm going to kill you," Evan repeated, choking on his own blood.

"Evan Tredioux is about to die an untimely death. Skydiving accident. You're not going anywhere. We're going to keep you as long as we need you."

Confusion swept through Evan as the needle pierced his neck. If there was one thing he knew better than anyone, it was skydiving. The swirl of the drugged haze filtered through his bloodstream and Evan swore retribution. They might be able to hold him captive but he'd eventually get out.

His captors? Dom Marretta? The people who bought the data? They were all dead men living on borrowed time.

They'd fucked with the wrong man and soon they'd all wish they'd never heard his name.

Evan's story will be continued in a future book installment in Club Altura Romance. If you enjoyed Hard Asset, the following books are available in this sexy romantic suspense series:

Solstice Burn (A Club Altura Romance Novella, Prequel)

Carnal Risk (A Club Altura Romance Novel, Book 1)

Wicked Rush (A Club Altura Romance Novel, Book 2)

Please enjoy two chapters of Carnal Risk, which is the first book in the Club Altura series.

◈ *Chapter One* ◈

Plummeting eighteen thousand feet brought the same rush it always did. Death was ever close, yet Garrett had never felt more alive. The deafening roar of the air cut into his mind. Not a cell of his body was left untouched by the adrenaline that pumped through his veins. Every single jump brought forth the clarity of not only his mortality, but his vitality.

As he passed through the clouds, Garrett spread his arms wide and pointed to his friend, Evan, who gave him a thumbs up. He glanced to his altimeter. *Twenty more seconds.* He let out a celebratory scream, exhilaration slamming through his limbs. *Ten seconds.* Spiraling recklessly through the air, the best part of the dive was coming to an end. *Five seconds.* Garrett smiled up at Evan, still holding out for one last moment. *One second.* He reached for the pull and with a pop, Garrett's chute exploded. The harness jerked him as the canvas ballooned open into the sky. Closing his eyes, he took a deep breath, descending like a feather from the sky. As he opened them, the breathtaking horizon of the beach came into view.

As he drifted through the wind, his heart seized as he glanced down to the field. A turbulent form whizzed past him through the air, and Garrett swore, his heart pounding as he watched his best friend plummet to his death. The chances of survival were infinitesimal. Hundreds of successful jumps and he'd never witnessed a fatal dive. He gasped for breath, aware that barring a miracle, Evan had already died.

Garrett's mind stormed with anger and grief. Like he'd been impaled by a knife, the reality of the accident speared through his chest. He was helpless, his descent stretching for what seemed like hours, and when his friend's body came into view, he fought the nausea. Tears came to his eyes as a gut-wrenching sob tore through his throat. *Evan, my friend. He's gone.* He couldn't comprehend how this could have happened, yet as grim faces below came into focus, he knew it could not be undone.

For years they had cheated death, victorious in achieving the ultimate high. Today, however, Garrett's world would come crashing down around him. As his feet touched the earth, he ran to embrace Evan. Tragedy rained down upon them and he cried up into the sky, devastated that his friend was forever gone.

ᴥ Chapter Two ᴥ

Garrett stared into the bottom of his scotch, its burn still fresh on his lips. Darkness crept into his soul, the grief consuming him. Fear wasn't a word in his vocabulary, yet he couldn't scrub the sight of his friend's lifeless body from his mind. *Unlucky.* That's what first responders had called it. Words like 'accident' and 'casualty' were tossed about, but he refused to accept their initial findings. Garrett had pressed the prosecutor's office for a special investigation, suspecting foul play.

As far as he was concerned, there was no such thing as luck. Strategy? Yes. Hard work? Most definitely. Accidents happened to other people, not Evan. Every single jump, he'd been meticulous when checking his rig. Some might even go so far as to call him obsessive compulsive, but Garrett knew it was what made him the very best. There was no fucking way he'd concede that his friend, the one who'd first taught him how to skydive, had simply succumbed to human error.

Garrett slammed his glass on the copper bar and slid it

toward the bartender, nodding at her. The perky blonde barkeep promptly brought the Macallan, poured two fingers and set the bottle in front of him. She gave him a sympathetic smile. As she turned around and bent over to give him an unobstructed view of her assets, he swore. Not even that perfect heart-shaped ass was enough to stir his dick. Garrett shook his head in disgust, aware he needed to get his shit together. As he ran his forefinger along the edge of his drink, a familiar voice caught his attention.

"Hey."

"You're late," Garrett responded, giving his friend a glare.

"Yeah fuck you too, G." Lars smiled at the bartender.

"Hi, baby. What can I get ya?" she asked.

Lars glanced to the whiskey that sat in front of Garrett. "A glass. We're taking the bottle."

"You sure about that now?" She raised a judgmental eyebrow at him.

"Yep, it's that kind of night." He shrugged. "Looks like you've started before me. You driving?"

"Nope. I've got a driver tonight." Garrett glanced to Lars, whose not so subtle eye roll told him he'd gone too far. "Is there a problem? No, don't answer."

The last thing he needed was a fucking lecture. Sensing one was coming, Garrett shoved out of his seat and snatched the decanter, gesturing to a secluded table in the corner. He sighed, settling into a well-worn leather chair and caught Lars' shadow flying by him, right before he took another swig of the amber liquid.

"Nice club," Garrett commented.

"Best jazz in the city. Got a special surprise I think you'll like."

"Oh yeah?" Garrett swirled the glass, never taking his eyes off the golden vortex.

"I thought you could use a distraction." Lars smirked, pouring himself a drink.

"That right, huh?"

"Listen, G, I know it's been a few weeks since..."

"Evan..."

"You and I both know this was no accident, but we've both got contracts to fulfill. Business goes on. It sucks, but if you don't start looking for his replacement, we can't..."

"What do you think I've been doing? I'm in the office. Day in. Day out. Even though Evan's not here, the world keeps spinning." Garrett gave Lars a sideways glance. "But I'm sure as hell not going to let it go. Something happened up there."

Over the years, Garrett had taken Emerson Industries from a garage start-up into a billion dollar corporation. Not only did Emerson's civilian suppliers count on timely shipments, government contracts needed to be fulfilled. Ongoing research and development took place on campus, ensuring the most advanced equipment in the world, and Evan had been a critical player in its success. Finding a suitable replacement for him was imperative, but it wouldn't be an easy task. Since the accident, Garrett had been operating in a daze, attending to small matters, but had neglected the critical infrastructure projects that needed intensive attention from a chief technology officer.

"Maybe, but you have to let the authorities handle it," Lars commented, his eyes falling onto the singer who'd stepped up on stage and picked up the microphone.

"I can't let it go. I've got to find out what happened. You know as well as I do that Evan used to be in the military – Airborne Division. He taught us all our shit. There's just no way he made a mistake. It's almost as if it's..." Garrett's words trailed off as he followed Lars' train of vision, the gorgeous creature capturing his attention.

The bar went silent as her golden voice resonated throughout the room. The jazz band transitioned into a sultry version of *You Put a Spell on Me,* and the seductive beauty stepped down from her perch, passing by a couple who sipped martinis. Garrett noted how she effortlessly weaved her way through the crowd of patrons, not allowing anyone to touch her. With a tantalizing flair, she turned her head toward Garrett and flipped her long blonde hair. The playful glint in her eyes told him she'd come for him next, a glimpse of desire hidden behind the violet contacts she wore. She stopped mid-song and slowly peeled away her gloves, tossing them into the crowd.

Lars laughed, and it was at that moment that Garrett realized he'd brought him here not just to distract him, but for a purpose. Momentary anger was promptly quelled as the blonde stepped out of a shadow. Her pale blue corset hugged her curves. Again she caught his gaze, slowly lowering the side zipper on her black pencil skirt. A drum solo began and the garment dropped to the floor, revealing ruffled panties. A cream-colored garter belt secured black thigh-high stockings. His cock jerked as she trailed her fingertips over her thighs, blowing a kiss to the quiet sophisticated crowd that continued to order drinks from passing waitresses.

Garrett wanted to be pissed at Lars, but he knew that his friend cared about him, how profoundly he'd been affected by Evan's death. It'd been months since he'd indulged in the fairer sex. Despite the temptation, he had no intention of initiating contact with the sultry performer.

The fragrance of her perfume drew him out of his contemplation, and through his peripheral vision, he spied his stealth singer. Tendrils of her hair brushed the back of his neck as she descended. Having given up on his resolve to show no interest, he glanced at Lars, whose eyes flashed to the entertainment. Delicate hands clutched his shoulders and Garrett slid his chair from the table to get a better view of her. His temptress ran her fingertips down his cotton shirt, causing his nipples to pebble in response. *Shit, I'm not here to fuck anyone*, he thought to himself as the blood rushed to his cock.

His eyes locked on hers as she straddled him, trailing her hands over his pecs. When her palms slid over his bare forearms, he fought the searing arousal that threatened his control. Garrett sucked a breath as she sat firmly on his lap, and her eyes snapped to his as they both registered his erection pressing through his jeans onto the thin fabric of her panties. It was in that moment that she gave him a small knowing smile. Rather than standing, she slowly tilted her hips, dragging her groin down the length of him. From a distance, no one would have seen. He resisted the urge to grab onto her waist. The fantasy of flipping her onto the table, tearing off the wet strip of nothing she called underwear and fucking her in front of the entire audience flittered through his mind, and he wondered if she'd like a little public action. The mere idea of it turned his dick into concrete, and he attempted to shift in his seat to relieve the growing ache.

If control was an Olympic sport, Garrett would hold a gold medal. Whether plunging out of a plane from eighteen thousand feet or plunging into a woman, his blood pressure never rose a single point. But despite his cool demeanor, Garrett failed to will his erection into submission. He took a slow breath, irked that a burlesque singer had cracked a sliver in his composure. He caught a glimpse of Lars, whose smile had faded. *Fuck me, he knows. Why the hell does it matter to him? Is he dating her? Yes, that's it. He knows her. Serves him the hell right for bringing me to this place.*

The lovely creature rose gracefully off him. Presenting her posterior like a meal on a plate, she arched her back and gestured to the black ribbons laced up the back of her corset. When he didn't respond, she abruptly sat on his thighs, jolting him back into his aroused state. She glanced back to him and grinned, tugging one of the strings. Her soft fingers met his, bringing them to the laces.

"I think that's good enough," Lars commented.

"What?" After this was over Garrett was going to kill Lars for fucking with him like this. He shook his head, confused as to what the hell was happening.

"A little help," she whispered, ignoring Lars.

Garrett noted that she'd turned her face away so he couldn't read her expression. He broke his resolve and began to pull open the tight threading, loosening the corset. He despised his body's lack of response to his demand to cease the arousal. His cock was harder than piling and the only relief he'd be getting tonight was from the palm of his hand.

The soft silky fabric brushed his hand as she pushed off him and made her way back to the stage. Holding her arms across her breasts, she stopped to wriggle her bottom, allowing the fabric to fall to her feet. As she turned for the big reveal, a velvet bra covered what the audience had expected to be bare. She wrapped both palms around the microphone, setting it back into the stand, and resumed her song. Like an angel, her alluring voice filled the room, and not a soul appeared disappointed that she hadn't bared more skin.

Garrett struggled to conceal his interest, aware that he should leave, but he sat captivated until the last note. A small chuckle drew his attention to Lars, who wore a broad grin.

"What's so funny?"

"You like her?"

"And? So what? She's beautiful. Moves well. Smells nice. Assertive...wasn't going to take no for an answer with that corset. What's not to like?"

"I'm glad you like her, I really am, but you might not want to sport that hard-on around her in the office," Lars said, nervously flexing his fingers.

"What the fuck is this about?"

"I'm about to help you is all."

"I saw the way she looked at you. What's going on between you and her?" Garrett asked, his voice tense. "And why exactly would I be seeing her in my office?"

"Just hear me out, bro."

"What did you do?"

"I didn't do anything. Just chill a second."

"Yet?"

"I know you, G. You're stuck on this thing with Evan," Lars noted.

"Thing? He's fucking dead," Garrett stated coldly.

"I hear you haven't even tried to replace him."

"What the hell did Chase say to you? You know what? I don't care what he said. The last time I checked, I ran Emerson. I don't need a babysitter." Garrett picked up his whiskey and glared at Lars. Of course he hadn't replaced Evan. No one could ever replace him. "You need to mind your own business. Seriously. Besides, whoever takes that position has to be one of us...someone I can trust implicitly. That's not gonna happen overnight."

"Exactly. And this is where she comes in."

"You're joking, right? The stripper?"

"Singer."

"Singer," he conceded. Garrett took a swig of his drink and set it forcefully down on the table.

"MBA. Wharton."

"Her?" His eyes darted to the stage. He watched with curiosity as she quickly wrapped herself up in a robe, concealing her costume. "So she's smart. So what? It's not enough. This isn't just some tech job. Evan had his hands in all sorts of shit. He was working on several major projects. There are so many requirements for whoever comes into his position it isn't even fucking funny. I'm not going to rush this."

"She's got clearances."

"Not enough." He glanced up and caught her staring at Lars. The flare in her eyes told Garrett that she wasn't happy with him.

"Listen. I've known her for ten years. She's the real deal. She's brilliant. Has rocked all my top accounts."

"What did she do for the government?" Garrett immediately wished he hadn't asked. There was no way this would work.

"Hacker. White Hat. She's in tune with problems our clients don't even know exist."

"Okay, great, well, we're very specialized. You know this. Does she jump?" He held up his hands to Lars as his friend glanced away. "No? Okay, great. What does she do? Does she do anything?"

"She's not so adventurous, but she can help you get the outsourcing project back on track, recruit for a permanent replacement," Lars responded, ignoring Garrett's question.

"What kind of a burlesque dancer doesn't actually take her clothes off?" Garrett paused, putting together the pieces of the puzzle. "Don't get me wrong, she was sexy, but it wasn't lost on me that the ending was a little anticlimactic."

"Give her a break. I just told you that she's a singer, not

a dancer. This is just kind of a hobby, anyway. It takes guts to get up and perform like that. She may be a little more cautious than most people, but she's working on it."

"Working on it?" He laughed.

"So she's a little repressed, okay? What the hell difference does it make, if she can do the job?" Lars asked with a sigh. "Listen, I promise you that she is what you need now. Yeah, you'll find someone to take Evan's position eventually but it's not going to be anytime soon. At least this way, you can keep things moving forward with our deal. Listen, you know I would not fuck with you. I'm telling you that she's the best. And she's tough. In fact, she's probably going to kick my ass for bringing you here."

"Why would she do that?" Garrett found it amusing that he'd misread the situation. Perhaps it hadn't been lust in her eyes; she'd been pissed at Lars. Whatever this meant to her, apparently it had been a secret and she wasn't at all pleased he'd mixed her worlds.

"She, uh, doesn't really want people to know she does this."

"Why did you bring me here then?"

"Because you need to get out and do something other than wallow in the office. And besides, if I'd told you about her without you actually seeing her sing, you'd have shot me down. This is the only thing she does that, you know, is risky."

"Risky? Are you high? I'd hardly call singing a song risky." Garrett laughed and rolled his eyes.

"You get up there, then, if you think it's so easy." Lars'

smile fell away as he grew angry with his friend's resistance. "Look, this is the deal. I can loan her to you. We just ended the Elkinson account. I moved a few people around. She may not be Evan, but she knows her shit. I know you're going to vet the hell out of her anyway, even though she already technically works in your network. Evan's death has been hard on all of us, but you've got to keep these deals moving. You need help, and I'm offering it to you. *She* is what you need."

"I need you to mind your own damn business." Garrett blew out a breath, staring at the bottom of his glass.

What Lars had said about her already being in the network was somewhat accurate. All the subsidiary corporations were independently owned, yet Garrett had a minority share within each, ensuring the viability of Emerson Industries. But clearances to work in the corporate building were a stricter, higher level, having access to covert government contracts.

Regardless of his opposition to Lars' suggestion, Garrett was aware that it could take months to find a suitable replacement for his chief technology officer. In the meantime, he'd been given a gift. A nice shiny one…very attractive and hard to resist. How he'd like to see what was underneath the wrapping she'd failed to peel away. Fuck it all, he knew he was thinking with his dick, but the temptation remained. It wasn't as if she'd really be his employee anyway.

"Two weeks. That's all she's got. If she doesn't add value, she's gone." Garrett shoved the chair out from the table and stood. "But if she screws up, she's out. I'm not in the business of taking on interns. If she doesn't hit the ground running, she's done. I'm not messing around."

"Good...because I don't want you messing around. We should, uh, maybe have some rules."

"You're kidding, right?"

"Come on, G. I know she's attractive but this is business. She's not like us."

"Yeah, I get that."

"She shouldn't come to our events."

"We haven't had any events since the accident."

"True, but she's not into jumps or any of our other extracurricular activities." Lars wiped his mouth with a cocktail napkin.

"I saw her looking at you. Are you fucking her?"

"Oh, no. Come on, man."

"Don't give me that shit. What's going on between you two?"

Lars shook his head.

"Spill it or we're done here." Garrett wasn't sure why it irritated him to think Lars had been intimate with her.

"We met in college. That's it."

"Anything else?"

"No, we didn't click that way. But we stayed friends over the years. She came on board five years ago."

"And you never brought her around? Ever?"

"No, she's not like us. Besides, you saw the look she gave me. Nothing's lost on you."

"She's pissed."

"Yeah, I just told you. I knew she did this, but I don't usually come to watch. So she's probably wondering why the hell I'm here."

"I'm sure she's going to love that she basically just had an interview with her new boss."

"Let's not get crazy now. I'm her boss. You have her on loan."

"This isn't going to work…"

"She's the best you're going to get, considering the circumstances."

Garrett just shook his head. *Yeah, I just undressed her while she ground on my cock. Great way to start a business relationship. Awesome.*

"What? She's not going to care that you were here."

"You're delusional. No wonder you can't keep a woman."

"Glass houses, bro." Lars shrugged. "There is one tiny thing…"

"What?"

"You can't fuck her. And before you go all CEO on my ass, this is a deal breaker."

"You're a dick, you know that. Why bring me here to see her like this?" Garrett raked his fingers through his hair in frustration.

"I told you. I brought you here so you could see her in her element, doing something that pushes her a little outside of her comfort zone. She's no jumper, but she's brave. If I hadn't done this, you wouldn't have ever considered her. You are sinking fast, my friend, and desperate times call for desperate measures. It worked. I got you to say yes." Lars set his palms on the table, his expression serious. "For years I've kept her away from that side of my life, away from you. She's my golden goose. I'm proud of her. There's nothing she does half-assed, including what she just did. I love you, Garrett, and because I love you, I'm not going to let you fuck up business. This thing with Evan...I can see how this is affecting you and I don't like it a damn bit. So I'm letting you borrow one of my finest assets. But I care about her, and because of that, she's off limits. Got it?"

"Fine. Whatever. Bring her to the office and we'll talk. I've gotta go. She stays two weeks, that's it."

"Two weeks," Lars repeated.

Garrett wasn't sure if he believed the words he was speaking but they sounded good. He caught the raised eyebrow Lars gave him, but ignored it. With a slap to his friend's shoulder, he saluted goodbye and headed toward the door. He hated that Lars sometimes knew him better than he knew himself. For the first time since Evan had died, he'd been distracted by something else, someone else.

Granted, he couldn't be sure whether or not she was going to be as good for his business as Lars promised. But considering his depression, he had to admit that for those few seconds she'd brushed against him, she'd taken his mind off of his grief. Despite his attraction, he'd promised Lars he wouldn't touch her. Garrett told himself it would be easy to ignore his feelings, and rationalized his arousal as temporary lust. A couple of weeks was all he needed to get the search for Evan's replacement on track. He'd put her in charge of the outsourcing deal, and she'd be in and out. Hopefully, he'd be able to stick to his word and not be in her.

Carnal Risk is available now!

Romance by Kym Grosso

The Immortals of New Orleans

Kade's Dark Embrace
(Immortals of New Orleans, Book 1)

Luca's Magic Embrace
(Immortals of New Orleans, Book 2)

Tristan's Lyceum Wolves
(Immortals of New Orleans, Book 3)

Logan's Acadian Wolves
(Immortals of New Orleans, Book 4)

Léopold's Wicked Embrace
(Immortals of New Orleans, Book 5)

Dimitri
(Immortals of New Orleans, Book 6)

Lost Embrace
(Immortals of New Orleans, Book 6.5)

Jax
(Immortals of New Orleans, Book 7)

Jake

(Immortals of New Orleans, Book 8)

Club Altura Romance

Solstice Burn

(A Club Altura Romance Novella, Prequel)

Carnal Risk

(A Club Altura Romance Novel, Book 1)

Wicked Rush

(A Club Altura Romance Novel, Book 2)

About the Author

Kym Grosso is the New York Times and USA Today bestselling author of the erotic paranormal series, *The Immortals of New Orleans*, and the contemporary erotic suspense series, *Club Altura*. In addition to romance novels, Kym has written and published several articles about autism, and is passionate about autism advocacy. She is also a contributing essay author in *Chicken Soup for the Soul: Raising Kids on the Spectrum*. In 2012, Kym published her first novel and today, is a full time romance author.

• • • •

Sign up for Kym's Newsletter to get Updates and Information about New Releases:

http://www.kymgrosso.com/members-only

Social Media/Links:

Website: http://www.KymGrosso.com
Facebook: http://www.facebook.com/KymGrossoBooks
Twitter: https://twitter.com/KymGrosso
Instagram: https://www.instagram.com/kymgrosso/
Pinterest: http://www.pinterest.com/kymgrosso/

Printed in Great Britain
by Amazon